HAPPY BIRTHDAY, CRYSTAL

BY **SHIRLEY GORDON**
PICTURES BY **EDWARD FRASCINO**

Harper & Row, Publishers

To Becky and Blair
Hank, Mike and Jami LaVoy

Happy Birthday, Crystal
Text copyright © 1981 by Shirley Gordon
Illustrations copyright © 1981 by Edward Frascino
All rights reserved. No part of this book may be
used or reproduced in any manner whatsoever without
written permission except in the case of brief quotations
embodied in critical articles and reviews. Printed in
the United States of America. For information address
Harper & Row, Publishers, Inc., 10 East 53rd Street,
New York, N.Y. 10022. Published simultaneously in
Canada by Fitzhenry & Whiteside Limited, Toronto.

Library of Congress Cataloging in Publication Data
Gordon, Shirley.
   Happy birthday, Crystal.

   Summary: Susan copes with jealousy when she meets
Crystal's other friend at Crystal's birthday party.
   [1. Friendship—Fiction]   I. Frascino, Edward.
II. Title.
PZ7.G6594Hap 1981   [E]   80-8941
ISBN 0-06-022006-6   AACR2
ISBN 0-06-022007-4 (lib. bdg.)

First Edition

There's a letter for me in the mailbox. It's
from Crystal. Crystal is my friend from school,
only she doesn't live by me.

I can always tell when it's a letter from
Crystal, because she draws funny cats all over
the envelope. When I tear open the letter, I
rip the tail of one of Crystal's funny cats.

Sorry, cat!

Crystal's letter says:

Yay, Susan!
Saturday is my birthday.
Can you come to my house?
I'm going to have a private party.

Love, Crystal

I run to tell my mother, "Saturday is Crystal's birthday. She wants me to come to her party."

Mother smiles. "That sounds like fun."

"I wish it was Saturday already!"

Crystal calls me on the telephone. "Don't forget my birthday party."

"Don't worry—I won't."

"It's going to be the best party I ever had."

"It's going to be the best party I ever went to."

"That makes us even," says Crystal.

Mother takes me shopping to buy a birthday present for Crystal. We look in all the stores, but I can't decide what to get.

4

"How about some pretty stationery? Crystal likes to write letters," my mother reminds me.

I smile. Now I know what I want to get for Crystal! I pull my mother inside a store where there is a row of little china cats sitting on a shelf.

"Crystal likes cats," I tell her.

I choose a cat for Crystal. It is polka-dotted and cross-eyed and has a crooked tail.

"Crystal likes *funny* cats," I tell my mother.

Saturday finally comes. I get dressed up in my favorite skirt and blouse and hair ribbon. Then my mother drives me to Crystal's house. I've never been to Crystal's house before.

"Ya-aay, Susan!" Crystal hollers when she sees me.

"Ya-aay, Crystal!" I holler back.

"Have a good time, girls," my mother calls as she drives away.

Crystal and I giggle at each other. We *always* have a good time.

Crystal takes me into her room. "I'll call up
Sherri and then we can get ready for the
party."
"Who is Sherri?" I ask her.
"Sherri is my friend who lives next door."
"Oh."
I didn't know Crystal had a next-door
friend. I wish *I* lived next door to Crystal.

Crystal goes to the window and hollers into her tin-can telephone. "C'mon over, it's time to get ready for my party."

I see someone in the window of the house next door. "I'll be right there!" she hollers back into her end of the tin-can telephone.

I wish I didn't always have to talk to Crystal on a *regular* telephone.

Crystal's cat is curled up on her bed. I sit
down and try to scratch his ears, but he gets
up and moves away from me.

"He doesn't know you yet," says Crystal.
"This is Susan, you silly cat," she tells him.

But he still won't let me scratch his ears.

"I brought you a birthday present." I give
Crystal the funny little china cat all wrapped
up in tissue paper.

Crystal puts it on her dresser. "It's not time
to open my presents yet. First, we have to
decorate my room for the party."

Crystal gets out some crepe-paper ribbons and a bag of bright-colored balloons. She climbs up on a chair and starts to hang the paper ribbons all over her room.

"I'll blow up the balloons for you," I tell her. I put a red balloon in my mouth, take a big breath, and blow. Nothing happens. I blow and blow as hard as I can.

"These balloons are too hard to blow up," I tell Crystal after I catch my breath.

Just then a girl runs in the door. "I'll go get
the bicycle pump," she says, and runs out
again.

"That was Sherri," says Crystal.

I take lots of big breaths and blow up three
balloons before Sherri gets back with the
bicycle pump.

Crystal introduces us. "Susan, this is Sherri.
Sherri, this is Susan."

"Hello. Your face looks like a purple
balloon," says Sherri.

I try to say "Hello" back, but I hardly have any breath left.

"Thanks for bringing over your bicycle pump," Crystal tells Sherri.

"It's *your* bicycle pump," says Sherri.

Crystal and Sherri laugh together. "Sherri and I borrow our things back and forth all the time," Crystal explains.

I wish *I* could borrow things back and forth with Crystal.

Sherri sits on Crystal's bed to pump up the balloons. Crystal's cat gets up beside her and lets Sherri scratch his ears.

Crystal stands on her tiptoes on top of the chair. "Somebody hand me the scissors."

"Where are they?" I ask.

"I know where." Sherri jumps up and gets the scissors out of Crystal's sewing basket. Then she gets some string out of Crystal's dresser drawer to hang up the balloons.

I've never been to Crystal's house before, so I don't know where anything is.

Crystal gets down from the chair and climbs up on the bed to hang more crepe-paper ribbons on the other side of the room.

"The decorations look super. *Crystal is a pistol*," Sherri sings.

"You helped me pick them out. *Sherri is the berries*," Crystal sings back.

15

I stand around, waiting for the party to
begin.

Finally, the room is all decorated. Crystal
jumps down off the bed. "Now we can get the
party on the road."

Sherri takes a package out of her jeans

pocket and gives it to Crystal. "It's your birthday present."

Crystal puts Sherri's present on her dresser next to mine. "It's not time to open my presents yet. First, we have to play Pin the Tail on the Hee-Haw."

I get out my hanky and give it to Crystal.
"You can use it as a blindfold."

Crystal ties it over her eyes and shakes her
head. "It's too skinny. You can see right
through it."

"My scarf will work better." Sherri ties her
scarf around my eyes. I can't see anything.

18

"Get ready. We're going to turn you around three times," Crystal warns me.

Crystal and Sherri turn me around three times. I feel dizzy. Everything is all black.

"Just feel for the wall. Straight ahead of you," Crystal whispers in my ear.

"No fair helping!" Sherri says.

"I don't need any help," I say. I walk straight ahead and bang *smack-dab* into the wall.

I reach out and pin the tail on the donkey. Crystal and Sherri laugh. I pull off the blindfold. My tail is hanging on the end of the donkey's nose!

I laugh, too. I don't want Crystal and Sherri to know how stupid I feel.

Sherri takes her turn and pins the tail on the donkey's leg. Then Crystal pins her tail on the donkey's stomach.

Their tails look silly—but not as silly as mine. "Susan wins the booby prize," says Crystal. She gives me a giant peppermint lollipop. "But don't start licking it yet. First, we have to have our ice cream and cake. I'll go get it."

HEE HAW!

"I'll help you," says Sherri.

They run out of the room together. Crystal's
cat jumps down off the bed and runs after
them.

I sit all alone in Crystal's room and stare at
the decorations. I wish I hadn't come to
Crystal's party!

Then Crystal sticks her head in the door.
"Hey, Susan—what're you sitting in here for?
The party's in the kitchen now."

21

I follow Crystal into the kitchen. Crystal and Sherri scoop up four dishes of ice cream—three mint'n'chip and one butter brickle. "For my cat," Crystal explains.

I stand around and watch.

"You guys take in the ice cream, and I'll bring in the cake," says Crystal.

I help Sherri carry the ice cream into
Crystal's room. She sets up the card table and
gets out the paper tablecloth and napkins,
because she knows where everything is.

Then Crystal brings in a chocolate cake with
chocolate frosting and thirty-six birthday
candles on top.

"That's how many there were in the box,"
she explains. "I didn't want to waste any."

Crystal puts the dish of butter brickle ice
cream down on the floor for her cat. "You
guys can light the candles while I think of my
wish," she tells us.

Sherri lights half the candles, and I light the other half.

"Now it's time to sing 'Happy Birthday to Me,'" says Crystal.

> *"Happy birthday, dear Crystal,*
> *Happy birthday to you."*

Crystal sings along with Sherri and me. "Three people can sing louder," she explains.

Crystal closes her eyes and makes a secret wish. Then she takes a big breath and blows all the candles out and all the paper napkins off the table.

After we eat our cake and ice cream, Crystal says, "*Now* it's time to open my presents."

She unwraps Sherri's present first. It's a little china cat just like *I* got for Crystal—only it's smooth and black and beautiful with green jeweled eyes.

"It's the best-looking cat I ever saw," says Crystal.

I feel awful. I wish I could take my present back and get Crystal something else. But she rips it open. "That's the *funniest*-looking cat I ever saw," she says.

She sets the cats side by side on top of her dresser. "Now I have a *collection*."

We play some more games, and I give
Crystal and Sherri some licks of my lollipop.
Then Crystal gets three pins out of her sewing
basket.

"Let's wind up my party with a *bang*," she
says.

We poke the pins in all the balloons.
BANG! BANG! BANG! BANG! BANG!

Beep-beep!

"What's that?" asks Crystal.

"It's my mother beeping her horn," I
explain. "I have to go home."

"That means my party's over," says Crystal.

"I'll stay and help you clean up," Sherri tells
Crystal. I wish *I* could stay and help Crystal
clean up.

Sherri waves good-bye. "So long, Susan.
Pleased to meet you."

"Thanks. You too."

Crystal's cat rubs against my leg and purrs. "He knows you now," says Crystal.

I give Crystal's cat a lick of my lollipop.

Crystal walks outside with me. "I wish I could tell you my birthday wish," she says, "but then maybe it wouldn't come true."

"I wish you and I lived closer," I say.

Crystal looks worried. "If somebody *guesses* your birthday wish, will it still come true?"

I smile at her. "Good ol' tee-legged, toe-legged, bow-legged Crystal."

"Yay, Susan, allaka-duzin'," says Crystal.

I get in the car and my mother drives away. Crystal stands on the sidewalk and waves and waves.

I roll down the window and holler, "Happy birthday, Crystal!" one more time.

rdon,

Birthday,